GRIZZLY BEAR FAMILY

by Audrey Fraggalosch

Illustrated by Donald G. Eberhart

For my dear dad — A.F.

Dedicated in memory of my best friend, Bill M., and to the loving support of my parents, Charles and Catherine E. — D.E.

Text copyright © 2000 Audrey Fraggalosch.
Book copyright © 2003 Trudy Corporation.

Published by Soundprints Division of Trudy Corporation, Norwalk, Connecticut.

Book design: Marcin D. Pilchowski
Editor: Laura Gates Galvin
Editorial assistance: Chelsea Shriver

First Edition 2003
10 9 8 7 6 5 4 3 2 1
Printed in China

Acknowledgments:
  Our thanks to Dr. Charles Jonkel of The Great Bear Foundation, Missoula, Montana, for his curatorial review.
  Donald G. Eberhart would like to give special thanks to Deborah Watkins for her time and research efforts on his behalf.

Library of Congress Cataloging-in-Publication Data is on file with the publisher and the Library of Congress.

GRIZZLY BEAR
FAMILY

by Audrey Fraggalosch
Illustrated by Donald G. Eberhart

Soundprints
Where Children Discover...

One gray day in January, a misty rain falls on the forest. Inside the hollow of a giant cedar tree, a grizzly bear rolls onto her back. Two tiny newborn cubs climb up on her warm belly. They hum happily as they nurse. Mother Bear gently licks her cubs before falling back asleep. The cubs snuggle close to their mother for the rest of the winter.

In the spring, the cubs follow Mother Bear outside into the rain forest.

Mother Bear is hungry after sleeping all winter long. She searches for fresh grasses and plants to eat. Sniffing the cool air, she smells skunk cabbage and heads for its bright yellow flowers. The cubs follow behind her. They nap nearby while she eats.

Rat-tat-tat! Rat-tat-tat! A loud hammering wakes the cubs from their nap! In an old dead tree, a woodpecker carves a nest hole with his strong bill.

Now the cubs are wide awake! They wrestle and tumble together on the soft, spongy moss that covers the forest floor. Mother Bear plays, too. She runs after the cubs in a game of tag.

Soon the cubs are big enough to follow Mother Bear along the trails of the rain forest.

Right in Mother Bear's path, a big male grizzly stands on his hind legs and rubs his back against a tree. Mother Bear knows that this huge male is dangerous. He could attack her cubs! She quickly turns around and leads her cubs away from the big grizzly bear.

When it is safe, the cubs follow Mother Bear down the trail to a beach.

Mother Bear stands up on her hind legs and sniffs for danger. She cannot smell another bear and she relaxes. Hungry, she leads her cubs to the water's edge to dig for clams and to look for crabs washed up by the tides.

Late in the summer, Mother Bear knows that it is time for the salmon to return to the river.

With her cubs by her side, she watches the bubbly surface of the water for splashes. Suddenly, she charges into the river and chases a salmon around and around. *Splash!* Eventually, Mother Bear grabs the wiggling fish in her mouth and brings it to the shore for her cubs to eat.

Many other animals gather at the river. Some days as many as twenty-five grizzly bears fish there. The biggest and strongest males get the best fishing spots, just below the waterfalls. Mother Bear carefully chooses a place away from the males. The cubs wait on the bank and watch her. She wades into the river and swims with her head under the water, "snorkeling" for salmon.

Mother Bear comes up for air and hears a sharp cry. One of her cubs is running away from a huge male grizzly! Mother Bear charges after the dangerous male. She lashes out at him, raking him with her long, sharp claws. He whirls around, snarling at her. This gives the cub just enough time to escape up a tree.

The male grizzly knows that he is no match for Mother Bear, and he wanders away.

During the last weeks of summer and early fall, the bears eat as much as they can to fatten up for the long winter.

When the trees lose their leaves and the heavy rains begin, Mother Bear leads her cubs through the forest and up the mountain, back to a winter den. They nibble on the last berries of the season.

Inside the den, Mother Bear shows her cubs how to rake together a thick nest of mosses and fallen leaves. Then the bears curl up next to each other and fall asleep.

Hoo-hoo, hoo-hoo! Outside, an owl hoots. The bears sleep through the night and the next day and night—and for most of the winter. They do not eat or drink, and they seldom leave their den.

In the spring, Mother Bear and her cubs slowly wake up and stumble outside. The bears wander among the tall ferns, licking up raindrops. Under a moss-covered log, a salamander looks for insects to eat. A hummingbird buzzes by and stops to drink nectar from a flower. The bears are hungry after so many months without food!

Mother Bear leads her cubs down to the river to feast on fresh greens and roots. The cubs will remember where and when to find these plants next spring. This summer they will learn how to fish and by next year, they will be ready to live on their own in the great grizzly forest.

THE GRIZZLY BEAR LIVES IN THE RAIN FORESTS OF THE PACIFIC NORTHWEST

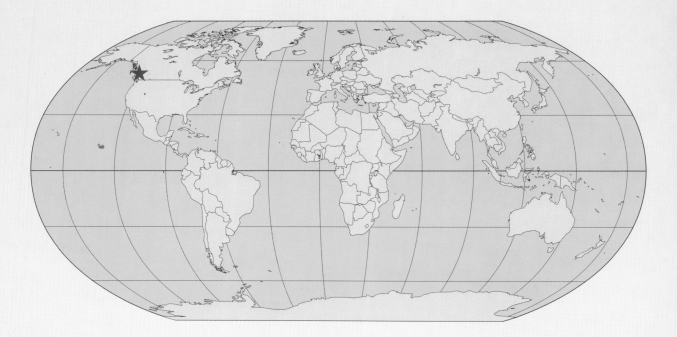

ABOUT THE GRIZZLY BEAR

Most grizzly bears are found in northern Canada and Alaska. Some of the largest male grizzly bears can weigh over 1,000 pounds and stand 9 feet tall! They can live more than thirty years in the wild.

Females usually give birth every three years. Two or three cubs are born in the hibernation den. The mother grizzly only wakes from hibernation to give birth and to care for her cubs.

Grizzly bears eat a variety of lush plants and many species of Pacific salmon.